The Nativity

Retold by JULIANA BRAGG

Illustrated by SHEILAH BECKETT

GOLDEN PRESS • NEW YORK

Western Publishing Company, Inc., Racine, Wisconsin

Copyright © 1982 by Western Publishing Company, Inc. Illustrations copyright © 1982 by Sheilah Beckett.
All rights reserved. Printed in the U.S.A. No part of this book may be reproduced or copied in any form
without written permission from the publisher. GOLDEN®, A GOLDEN STORYTIME BOOK®, and GOLDEN PRESS®
are trademarks of Western Publishing Company, Inc. Library of Congress Catalog Card Number: 81-84380
ISBN 0-307-11960-2/ISBN 0-307-61960-5 (lib. bdg.)   B C D E F G H I J

ong ago, in a dusty hillside village called Nazareth, there was a young woman named Mary. Her family and her people were poor, and there was trouble throughout their land.

Every day Mary helped her mother, cleaning their
small clay house, baking the bread, and washing the clothes.
When she went to the village well for water, she had a few
moments to talk with her friends. Mary's life was just like
that of most young women in Nazareth, and she was content.

But God had a plan that was going to change her life forever. God had promised to send a messiah—a chosen leader who would show his people the way to a better, happier life. For many years, the people had waited and longed for the Messiah.

And now it was time for him to come.

One day an angel appeared to Mary.
How fiery bright and beautiful he was!

"Greetings, Mary," said the angel. "I bring you
good news. God has chosen you to be the mother
of his son. You are to name the baby Jesus. He shall be
a great man—the one who will save all people."

At first Mary was troubled. Could it be true?
Had God really chosen a simple peasant girl to be
the mother of his son?

Then she looked at the angel and knew that what
he said was true. "I will do whatever God asks of me,"
she said, and she was filled with joy.

After that day, Mary still carried water from the well.
She still mended the family's clothes and made round,
flat loaves of bread for supper. But now everything seemed
different to her because, in her body, the son of God
was growing. She often smiled to herself as she worked.

Only Joseph, the man she was soon going to marry, knew the reason for her smile. An angel had come to him in a dream to tell him that Mary would be the mother of God's son.

When it was nearly time for the baby to be born, a message came to all the people from the ruler of the land. It said that every man must go to the village where he was born to pay a special tax. Joseph would have to make a trip to Bethlehem, his home village.

Mary went too, riding on a donkey, with Joseph
walking by her side. It was a long journey, over
steep and rocky hills. There were few places along
the way to stop and rest. Joseph and Mary were very
tired when they finally arrived in Bethlehem.

The little village was crowded with travelers who had come to pay their taxes. All the homes and inns were full. And now Mary felt that the baby would be born very soon. Where would Joseph and Mary find shelter?

At last someone led them to a small stable.
It was just a cave in the hillside. But it was a place
that was warm and dry and out of the wind.

And there, in that small stable, the baby Jesus
was born.

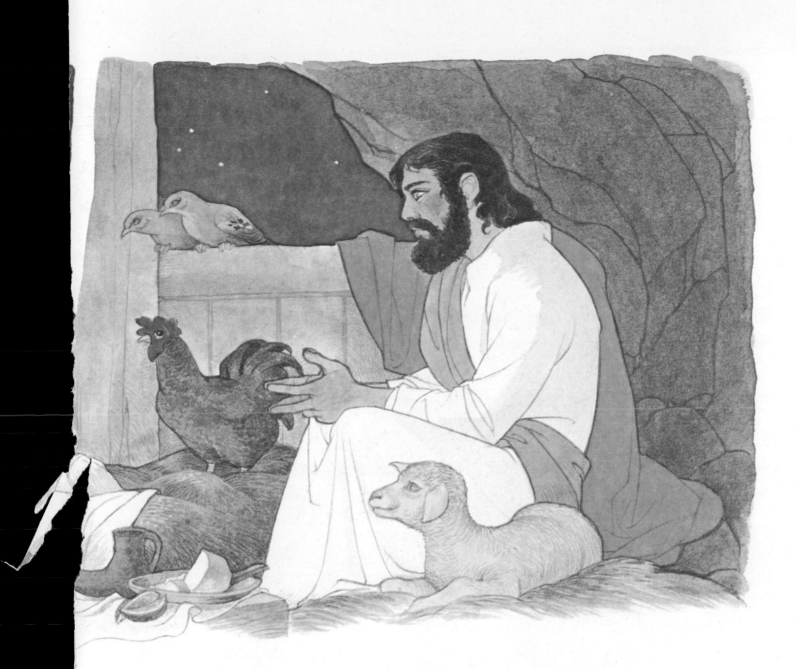

Mary wrapped her baby in a blanket she had made.
Joseph filled a manger with straw and they laid
the baby in it.

That night there were shepherds in the fields near
Bethlehem. As they watched their flocks, a great light
shone all around them and an angel appeared.

The shepherds did not know what was happening.
They fell to the ground and were very frightened.

But the angel said, "Do not be afraid. I bring you
wonderful news. Tonight, in Bethlehem, a child is born
who is the Messiah. Go there and look for a baby lying
in a manger."

And the sky was suddenly filled with angels, singing
and praising God.

Then as suddenly as they had come, the angels
disappeared. The shepherds talked excitedly about what
the angel had said. Had the Messiah really come at last?
They gathered up their things and hurried to Bethlehem.

There they found Mary and Joseph and the baby.
Jesus looked just like any other new baby. And yet
the shepherds could feel how very special he was.
So they rushed away to tell everyone the good news.

Alone in the stable, Mary held the baby Jesus in her
arms. She wondered how different her life would be as
God's plan for her and Joseph and Jesus continued to unfold.
One thing she knew certainly. She was going to be
a very special mother to this baby. For he was the Messiah,
the son of God, and she loved him with all her heart.